D1072739

Juniper Jupiter

World's Greatest Juggler

BY CHERRY SMITH

To my loving parents,

who made my dream come true.

COURIER PUBLISHING

Juniper Jupiter
wanted to be
the best
at everything!

In school, Juniper's hand
was always the first
raised, even when she
didn't know the answer.

In music class, she sang loudest, because she thought louder meant better.

In gym class, Juniper always ran the extra mile, because she had to win every race (even when she felt tired and out of breath).

In art class, she made the biggest art projects, because she thought the bigger the artwork, the better.

Being the best at everything takes a lot of hard work. For Juniper, this meant having a lot of work to take home — big chapter books to read, art projects to complete, music to practice and laps to run.

It's good to dream big, work hard and set high goals for yourself. It's not good when it becomes too much work and nothing gets done. That's what happened to Juniper.

Juniper strapped on her overstuffed book bag and walked home from school. She looked like a camel with one large hump.

At home, she went straight to her room. Toys, books, clothes and piles of all sorts of things were scattered around. Her space was a mess. She stood in a three-foot-tall clothes pile, feeling very overwhelmed by it all. Frustrated, she picked up two books and tossed them above her head.

She reached out her hands and caught both books before they hit the floor.

"Hmmm," she thought, "I wonder if I can catch more."

She picked up a shoe, a
hairbrush, a hat, a stuffed
bear, and a bottle of glue.
All of the objects went up.
To her surprise, she caught
everything and kept it all
moving in the air. A grip and
a swift lift with her hands
kept all five objects rotating
— like a Ferris wheel!

In a few short minutes, Juniper Jupiter became a juggler. She picked more and more things off the ground and juggled the items in the air. She felt good when she saw less mess on her floor, and she felt proud of her newfound juggling talent.

She juggled
at sunup ...

She even showed off her remarkable talent at recess by juggling three Frisbees and eight balls. Her friends watched in amazement.

She juggled more
schoolwork, too!
She tossed heavy
chapter books, art
projects, musical
instruments and
running shoes.
She continually
kept them spinning
around and around.

One day, her hands that were once so quick lost their grip on all of the things spinning around, and they all came crashing down. No longer could Juniper juggle everything. She stared at her messy room. This mess was more than she could juggle. Piece by piece, she cleaned her space.

Proudly, she stood on her clean floor. From now on, she would only juggle one thing at a time. Then she picked up one small rubber ball, tossed it high up in the air and caught it. This made her very happy!

9 781940 645568